This Little Princess

story belongs to

.O.L.i.V.i.a. . . . .

This paperback edition first published in 2015 by Andersen Press Ltd.

First published in Great Britain in 2015 by

Andersen Press Ltd., 20 Vauxhall Bridge Road, London SW1V 2SA.

Published in Australia by Random House Australia Pty.,

Level 3, 100 Pacific Highway, North Sydney, NSW 2060.

Copyright © Tony Ross, 2015.

The rights of Tony Ross to be identified as the author and illustrator of this work

have been asserted by him in accordance with the Copyright, Designs and Patents Act, 1988.

All rights reserved. Colour separated in Switzerland by Photolitho AG, Zürich.

Printed and bound in Malaysia by Tien Wah Press.

1 3 5 7 9 10 8 6 4 2

British Library Cataloguing in Publication Data available.

ISBN 978 1 78344 291 1

A Little Princess Story

I Feel Sick!

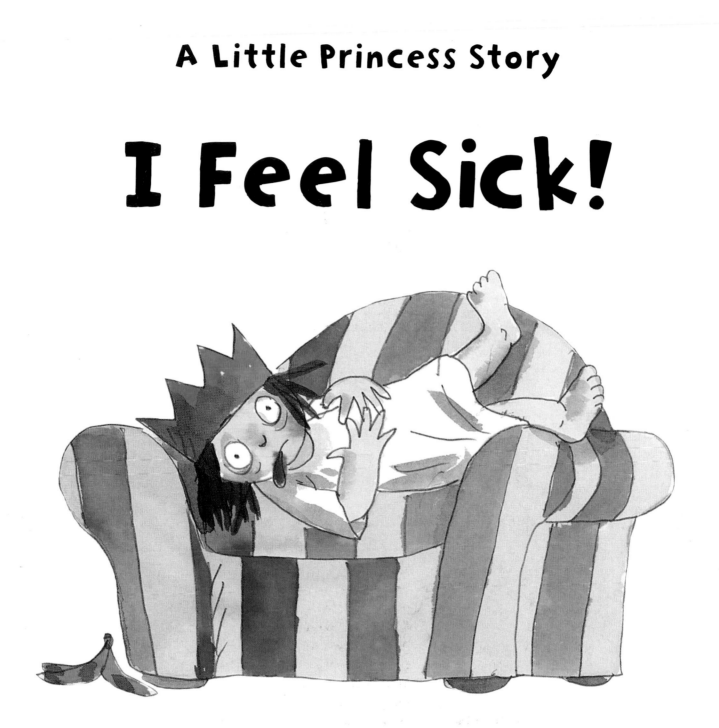

Tony Ross

Andersen Press

The Little Princess was never sick.

Except when anyone asked her to do something.

"Why not take Scruff for a walk?" said the King.

"Ooooh, I feel sick!" said the Little Princess.

"Can you help me clean out the cat's tray?" asked the Queen.

"I'd really enjoy that," said the Little Princess. "But I feel sick!"

"Will you help me teach my horse to jump?" asked the General.

"I would love to help," said the Little Princess. "But I feel sick!"

The Little Princess felt most sick when it was time to go to school.
"You don't *look* sick," said the Queen.

So the Little Princess painted her face green.

"I can hardly walk," she said. "I feel so sick!"

"Eat vegetables for dinner, that's the thing!"
said the Doctor. "Lots of greens will make you less green."

"I feel too sick to eat any dinner," said the Little Princess.
"But I might just manage a few jelly babies."

One day, when the Little Princess felt far too sick to do anything at all, the postman brought her a letter.

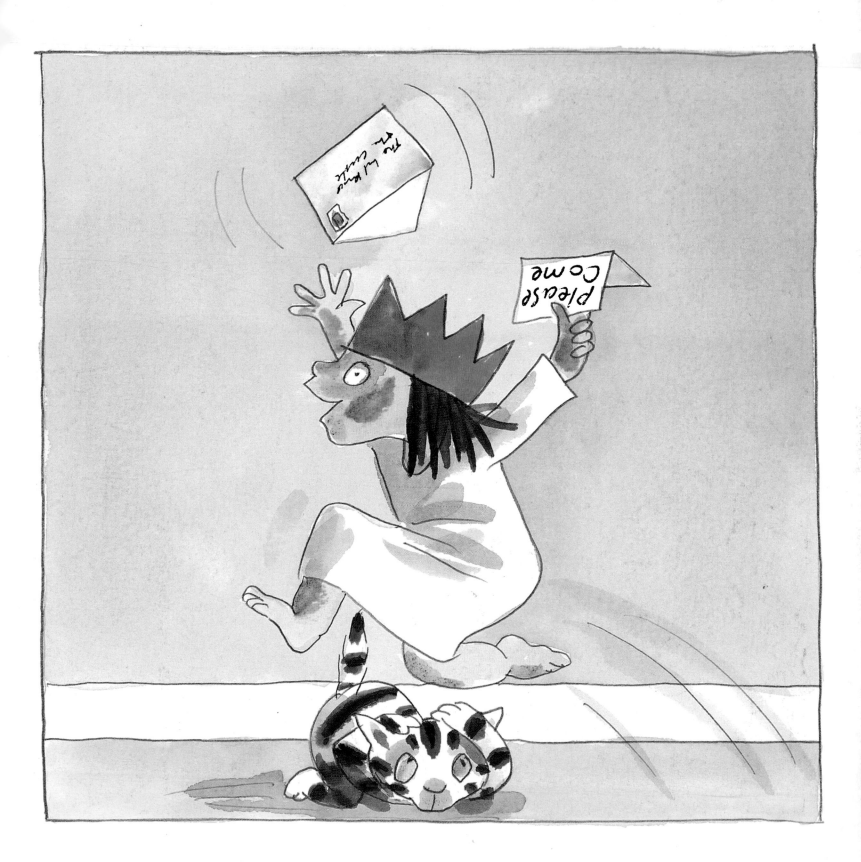

"Ooooh!" she squealed. "It's an invitation to Molly's party!"

"Pity you can't go," said the Queen. "You feel too sick."

"I feel MUCH better now!" said the Little Princess.

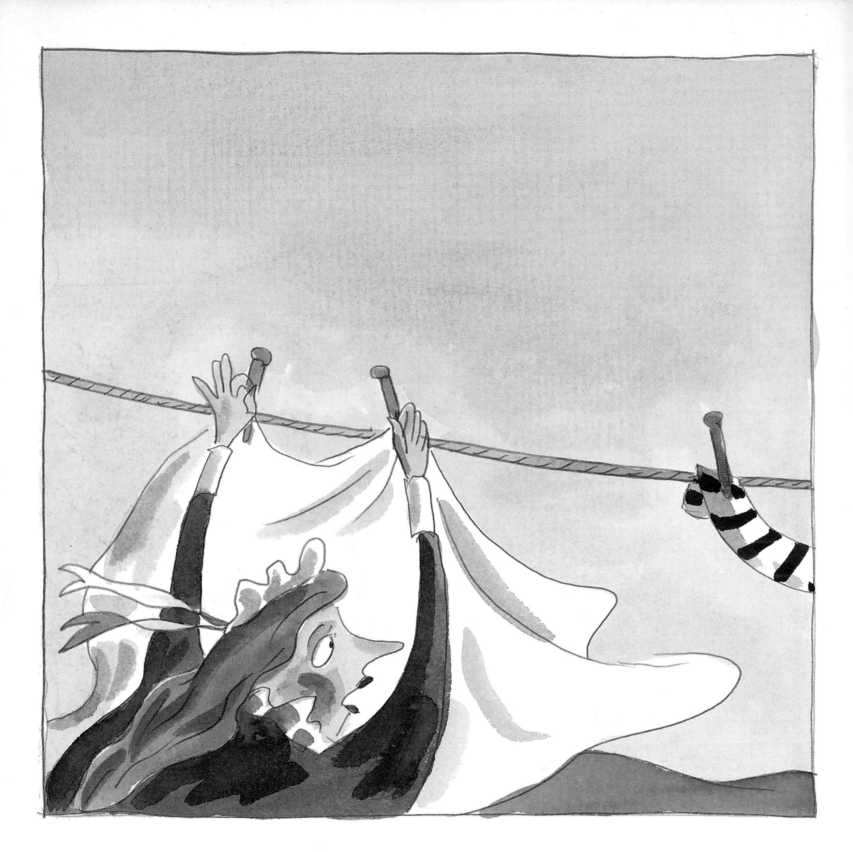

The day of the party arrived. The Little Princess felt so excited.
"Don't you feel sick?" asked the Maid.

"No," said the Little Princess. "I feel WONDERFUL!"

The party was fun and there was so much to eat!

There were games to play and lots of dancing...